FANGS
VAMPIRE SPY

WITHDRAWN
FROM
STOCK

The Fangs, Vampire Spy, series

FANGS

VAMPIRE SPY

OPERATION: GOLDEN BUM

TOMMY DONBAVAND

WALKER BOOKS

First published in 2013 by Walker Books Ltd
87 Vauxhall Walk, London SE11 5HJ

10 9 8 7 6 5 4 3 2 1

This book has been typeset in Helvetica and Journal

Printed and bound in Great Britain
by Clays Ltd, St Ives plc

British Library Cataloguing in Publication Data:
a catalogue record for this book is available from the British Library

ISBN 978-1-4063-3158-5

www.walker.co.uk

www.fangsvampirespy.co.uk

For Arran, who shares certain ...
abilities with the Great Disgusto

MPI Personnel

Agent Fangs Enigma
World's greatest vampire spy

Agent Puppy Brown
Wily werewolf and Fangs's super sidekick

Phlem
Head of MP1

Miss Bile
Phlem's personal
secretary

**Professor
Hubert Cubit,
aka Cube**
Head of MP1's
technical division

Special Agent Fangs Enigma – the world's greatest vampire spy – adjusted his sunglasses and calmly spun the wheel of the jet-black speedboat, sending plumes of spray over the children playing on the riverbank. They watched in awe as the boat roared off in pursuit of a larger, green-coloured vessel.

Fangs flicked his tongue against one of the two pointed teeth jutting from his upper jaw. It began to glow a bright, shimmering blue. "This is Enigma," he barked, turning the wheel sharply to avoid capsizing a local fisherman. "Target is in sight."

A tinny voice sounded from his other fang.

8

"Good of you to check in at last. I was beginning to think you'd forgotten all about us." It was Phlem, Fangs's boss and the head of Monster Protection, 1st Unit, aka MP1.

Enigma snarled.

"Can you confirm the identity of the prey?" Phlem continued.

"Puppy...?" Fangs said, without so much as a backwards glance. "Can you assist?"

Puppy Brown, a werewolf and fellow MP1 agent, typed a few commands into her laptop computer, and an image, projected directly from Fangs's sunglasses, appeared on the screen. After zooming in on the sole occupant of the speedboat they were chasing, she ran his scarred features through the facial-recognition software. The result was displayed almost immediately.

"It's Zed," she announced.

Fangs tongued his blue tooth to switch the line of communication back to MP1 Headquarters.

"Target confirmed as the zombie Zed," he said. "Permission to apprehend?"

"Permission granted," came the reply from Phlem, "but try to keep the destruction down to a minimum this time, please!"

With a wry smile, Fangs pressed down on the accelerator. The boat picked up speed, and his long, black cape whipped out behind him in the breeze.

A look of panic flashed in the zombie's eyes as the MP1 speedboat pulled up alongside his vessel. After grabbing his shoe, he ripped his entire foot off at the ankle and hurled it at Fangs. The appendage bounced off the vampire's head with a sickening thump.

Puppy leapt to her feet. "Are you OK, boss?" she asked.

The vampire cricked his neck from side to side. "Just *toe*-rrific," he quipped. "But *heel* pay for that! Take the reins..."

Still rolling her eyes at her boss's bad joke,

Puppy grabbed the steering-wheel as Fangs stepped up to the edge of the boat, gripping his cloak tightly with his long, sharp fingernails. "Are you sure about this, boss?" Puppy asked.

"He hasn't got a *leg to stand on*," Fangs growled before leaping off the boat. His cape stiffened and he sailed across the churning water to land with ease beside the startled zombie.

Fangs's fist made contact with Zed's nose, splitting it open and sending plumes of black snot flying everywhere. The vampire ducked to avoid being covered by gunk, and Zed took the opportunity to wrap his green, decaying hands around his opponent's throat.

Fangs Enigma's usually white face paled even more as the zombie bared his few remaining teeth and hungrily eyed a pulsing vein. "Let's see 'ow you like bein' bitten, vampire!" Zed snarled.

Fangs jumped to one side, accidentally pressing against the accelerator. The boat lurched forward and clipped a buoy. The zombie staggered and let go of Fangs's throat. "Puppy! Now!" Fangs yelled.

The werewolf grabbed a length of rope from the deck of her boat, tied a quick loop and then spun it around her head. She howled with delight when the rope caught first time, landing over Zed's head and shoulders. "Get ready, boss!" she shouted, pulling the rope as hard as she could—

And the zombie's head came off.

Fangs was still staring in horror at the stump of spine protruding from Zed's neck when the boat careered into the riverbank and shot out of the water like a rocket.

Puppy's lasso had slipped off the headless corpse and caught round the boat's gearstick. She pulled it taut with a deafening *TWANG*! The boat was too heavy, though, and Puppy was dragged off her feet and sent flying through the air behind the still-fighting vampire and zombie.

Meanwhile, in the water below, the sleek, black MP1 speedboat smashed into a bridge and exploded in a searing hot ball of flame…

TOP SECRET

MP1 Mission File #1

Codename: Golden Bum

Report by: Agent Puppy Brown

I swung the pack over my shoulder and hurried
to catch up with Fangs. He was several paces
ahead of me, striding towards the statue of
Winston Churchill, which stood in front of the
Houses of Parliament.

"Cheese!"

I glanced round to see a family of Egyptian mummies having their photo taken in front of the famous building and then had to dodge to the side as a group of zombie school kids ran to catch a bright-red tour bus. Another typical day in London.

We reached the Churchill statue just as Big Ben struck midday. At the sound of the famous bell, everyone in the square turned to look at the clock tower and Fangs took the opportunity to press his palm against a hidden sensor on the base of the statue. A secret panel slid down to reveal a staircase beyond. We were descending deep below London before the fourth *BONG*!

An egg-shaped monorail car was waiting at the bottom of the stairs. Fangs disabled the self-destruct mechanism, designed to stop intruders, and we were soon whooshing silently beneath the River Thames.

This is what my life has been like for the past three months, ever since I was teamed up with

Agent Fangs Enigma. Although, to be fair, things haven't been exactly normal since I first became a werewolf.

You've probably read stories about spooky creatures like vampires and werewolves. Well, guess what? They're all true. Supernatural creatures do exist. They have just spent centuries hiding away in dark castles and mouldy dungeons because humans kept attacking their homes, armed with pitchforks and flaming torches. But that's all history now. Ever since the supernatural equality laws were passed, people of all shapes and sizes have lived happily side by side.

Well, almost everyone. Just like in the human world, the supernatural one has its fair share of bad guys, and it's the job of MP1 to track them down and catch them – to protect the world from the very worst criminal *monster*minds. And that's where I come in...

You probably know the legend: werewolves are

perfectly normal people – apart from every full
moon when they change into terrifying wolves.
But that's not how it works with me. Something
went wrong with my first transformation and
I ended up permanently stuck as a werewolf –
claws, fur, fangs, the lot.

My parents were, of course, surprised to
suddenly have a supernatural creature in the
family – especially such a hairy one. There were
a couple of werewolves in my school, but unless
you happened to be with them at full moon, you
never saw them as wolves. I'm the exact opposite.
The full moon is the *one* night a month when
I change back into a goofy schoolgirl. I was a
laughing-stock.

My mum and dad did their best to help, by
shaving my arms and legs every morning in an
effort to make me look like a "normal" person.
It didn't fool anyone. I looked like a chihuahua in
a dress.

Then I was recruited by MP1 – and suddenly I wasn't just an overly hairy kid. I was Puppy Brown, trainee secret agent!

"Puppy!" Fangs's voice jerked me back to the present.

We had arrived at HQ.

"FANGSH! IT'SH YOU!" screeched an adoring

voice as we stepped into one of MP1's sleek offices.

Miss Bile is the big guy's secretary and has a

major crush on my vampire boss.

I feel sorry for her. She's definitely not Fangs's

type. Besides, it can't be easy for a middle-aged

banshee to lose all her teeth. It has made talking

20

very difficult. Mind you, *listening* to Miss Bile is no picnic either and I am always wiping globs of spit off my fur when I come to deliver paperwork. There's a rumour that an agent called Sissy Soss resigned after nearly drowning during Miss Bile's half-hour briefing on stage-six state secrets.

Fangs whipped off his cloak, tossed it onto the coat rack and flashed the banshee a wicked smile. This was too much for Miss Bile, and she fainted, face first, onto her desk – accidentally sending off a half-written email about goblins and stapling her tongue to a pile of receipts.

I was dragging the banshee back into her chair when a voice gurgled through the speaker phone on the desk. "Enigma! Is that you?"

Phlem, the head of MP1, didn't sound happy. But then he never is. Meeting him for the first time is quite an experience. People say he's the only swamp beast ever to have survived away from the murky depths of the legendary black lagoon.

"Drink?" he slobbered as Fangs and I entered his office next door.

"Thank you," said my boss, easing himself into an armchair. "I'll have milk with a dash of blood."

I watched as the head of the greatest supernatural counter-intelligence organization in the world frothed up a glass of milk with a whisk and then added a few drops of human blood from a decanter. After spotting the tendrils of slime coating the glass he handed to Fangs, I declined a drink of my own.

Phlem took a long sip of his favourite cocktail – frogspawn on the rocks – and glared across his desk at us. "Do you know how much trouble you two caused in Istanbul?" he said. "We're having to replace two minarets on the Blue Mosque and rebuild an entire spice market!"

"I know how much trouble we *saved* the local community from by bringing Zed to justice," Fangs replied.

"That's another thing," bubbled Phlem. "Why isn't Zed in the cells?"

"I can answer that, sir," I said, untying my pack. "Only Fangs and I survived the boat crash to any real degree..." I angled the bag to show him the collection of rotting zombie body parts inside. "We weren't quite sure what to do with him."

Phlem sighed – it sounded like someone emptying a bath of custard. "Get him down to the medical bay," he ordered. "They can stitch him back together and then you can put him in the cells."

Fangs drank the last of his milk, his tongue lapping hungrily at the drops of blood at the bottom of the glass. "Will that be all, sir?" he asked.

"You don't get off that easily, Agent Enigma,"
barked Phlem. "Our contacts in Turkey say Zed
was over there to buy supplies for a wizard..."

My hairy brow creased with interest.
"A wizard, sir?"

"Yes, Brown," said Phlem. "A wizard we're
certain was involved in the robbery at a dinner
party at the German Consulate last week. Every
single guest blacked out at the same moment, and
when they came round, all their belongings were
missing."

"What made them black out?" I asked.

"That's the problem – no one seems to know."

"But you think this wizard might be involved?"
said Fangs.

Phlem nodded. "We don't know much about
him. He hasn't shown up on our radar before.
All we have is a single picture of him, caught by
the German Consulate's CCTV shortly before the
robbery." He pressed a button on his computer and

a photograph was projected onto the office wall behind us. A photograph of quite possibly the most hideous-looking person I'd ever seen – and I work for a disgusting swamp beast!

The wizard's skin was pockmarked with scars and spots, and his small, beady eyes were so close together that they almost met in the middle. Add to that a broken nose and thin, twisted lips, and you've got a face you'd  never forget – no matter how hard you tried.

Fangs was the first to comment. "Looks like the ugly club's got a new president." He smiled. "Where's he based?"

"We've no idea," admitted Phlem. "We're hoping Zed can shed some light on the German Consulate robbery and then tell us whatever else his wizard boss may be planning."

"What's the wizard's name?" I asked.

"We couldn't find his real identity on file anywhere," said Phelm. "Just the professional wizard name he goes by." The slime beast downed the rest of his drink. "He calls himself the Great Disgusto!"

Fangs led the way through the maze of corridors and secret testing rooms that make up MP1 Headquarters until we reached the medical bay.

The whitewashed room was filled with stainless-steel tables and trays of pristine yet lethal-looking medical equipment. Padlocked cabinets held medicines of every description, and the walls were covered in posters featuring graphic images of almost every disease known to man or monster – plus a couple of particularly nasty ones that weren't yet public knowledge.

Fangs rapped a scalpel against a specimen jar, making the glass ring like a bell. "Shop!" he called out. "Who's on duty around here?"

A surgeon in a long smock, face mask and surgical cap appeared in the doorway to the operating theatre. "Can I help you?"

"We want this miscreant put back together," said Fangs, untying the bag and dumping its decomposing contents all over a nearby table. "He went to *pieces* when I arrested him."

The doctor examined the various zombie parts. "This could take some time, and it won't be easy..."

"You can do it, though?" I asked.

"Of course," said the surgeon, pulling off the cap and face mask.

Fangs stared as long blonde hair tumbled free, falling down to frame a beautiful female face with piercing blue eyes. "Wait a minute," he cried. "You're a woman!"

Never let it be said that my boss isn't observant.

The surgeon removed her baggy surgical gown to reveal a slender dress. "I'm also the new head of this department. Doctor Olga Nowkoff." She held out a perfectly manicured hand for my boss to shake, but instead he lifted it up and delicately kissed it.

"The name's Enigma," he crooned. "Fangs Enigma."

I sighed. If my boss has one weakness, it's beautiful women – and Doctor Nowkoff was as gorgeous as they come.

"You haven't told me what time you get off work, doctor," Fangs went on.

"No," agreed Doctor Nowkoff. "I haven't." She selected a long needle from a tray of equipment and threaded it with a length of artificial ligament. Fangs gazed at her lovingly as she began to reattach the henchman's limbs. I knew my boss would stay in adoration mode for a while, so I took the opportunity to search Zed's jacket for evidence.

"I've got some grains of something here, Fangs," I said, pulling a few flecks of brown dust from one of the pockets.

"What is it?" Fangs asked, barely taking his eyes off the doctor.

"I'm not sure. It could be gunpowder – although..." I held the tiny specks up to my snout and sniffed. "It smells like ... mushrooms!"

"Mushrooms?" repeated Fangs.

I nodded. "May I use one of your microscopes, Doctor Nowkoff?"

The doctor gestured towards a bench. "Help yourself."

I quickly scattered the grains onto a glass slide

and looked at them through the lens of a powerful electron microscope.

"It *is* mushroom," I announced.

After flipping open my laptop, I found an online database of fungi, yeasts and moulds. I sifted through the entries until I found a match. "It's a type of mushroom called tigertop, or *Tricholoma pardinum*."

My boss didn't appear to be impressed or even interested. He was too busy blowing softly into Doctor Nowkoff's ear.

"Are you listening to me, Fangs?" I demanded.

He jumped at the sound of his name and accidentally spat a glob of spit onto the doctor's neck. Thankfully, she was so absorbed in reattaching one of the zombie's arms that she didn't notice.

"Of course I'm listening!" Fangs hissed while trying to subtly wipe the spit away with his cloak. "What's so special about Zed having bits of mushroom in his pocket? He might have been making himself a pizza."

"Whatever he wanted tigertop for, it wasn't lunch," I said. "It's poisonous and will give you a very bad stomach for several days after eating it."

"Well, this suspect hasn't eaten any mushrooms," Doctor Nowkoff said, picking up what looked like a deflated balloon. "His stomach is completely empty."

A smile crept across Fangs's face as he took a step closer to the doctor. "My stomach's empty, too." He smirked. "Perhaps we should go to dinner and fill it up. Somewhere cosy, where there isn't *mushroom* between us..."

The eyes on Zed's severed head flickered open. "Give the lovey-dovey stuff a rest, Enigma," he groaned. "I'm going to have a hard time being sick if I don't know where my throat is."

"I wouldn't make the stitching too secure, doctor," Fangs snarled. "I may have to tear him back into bits to get the information I need about the Great Disgusto."

"Do your worst, funny fangs," spat Zed. "I won't tell you a thing."

As Fangs sneered at the zombie, I picked up the henchman's jacket again and felt a slight lump in the fabric beneath my claws as I did so. On further examination, I discovered that it was the zip for a hidden pocket – and inside was a single tooth. "This looks too clean to be one of Zed's," I said.

Fangs leaned closer to the bits of zombie on the table. "What's the deal, Zed?" he asked. "Why are you carrying poisonous mushrooms and teeth around?"

"I'm saying nothing," Zed said.

"Then I'll find a way to *make* you tell me what I want to know," said Fangs.

"You can't if I'm not able to talk." One of the zombie's hands jumped up onto its fingers and scuttled along the metal table to its head. Then it reached inside Zed's mouth and, before anyone could stop it, ripped the entire rotting tongue out and tossed it into the far corner of the room.

"This is a waste of time," I said. "We'll get more answers if we take the tooth down to the lab."

"In a moment," said Fangs. "I just have to get Doctor Nowkoff to check my lips first. They're suffering from a lack of kisses." He closed his eyes and pursed his lips in the doctor's direction.

"Well, we can't have that, can we?" soothed Doctor Nowkoff. With a smile, she lifted Zed's head up by the hair and pressed the zombie's rubbery lips to my boss's mouth.

They say people heard the scream over a mile away.

Professor Hubert Cubit is MP1's top brainbox –
in more ways than one.

Early on in life, the professor realized that facts
and information only ever come in square things.
"Books, computers, filing cabinets – all square and
all filled with knowledge," he told me during my
first week of training. "Tennis balls, potatoes and
scoops of ice cream – all round and hardly any
knowledge in them at all."

Determined that he would also be stuffed with information, the young Hubert built a tight-fitting wooden box to wear like a hat at all times, so changing the shape of his head as it grew, from a useless sphere to a fact-filled square. It is for this reason that he is now known within MP1 as "Cube".

Fangs paced the laboratory as Cube studied the tooth under his microscope. "Very interesting..." the professor muttered.

"What is?" asked Fangs.

Cube peered over the top of his square glasses. "Why, the tooth, of course! We may not have been able to find a match in the dental-records database, but that doesn't mean it can't lead us to its owner."

"Was I right?" I asked. "It's not one of Zed's, is it?"

"No, it's not," replied Cube, scratching the corner of his scalp. "The enamel is in good condition, and it contains faint traces of magic."

"Magic?" I said. "So it could be the tooth of a wizard – like the Great Disgusto?"

"That is quite possible, yes."

"Knowing that still doesn't help us, though," Fangs pointed out. "Even if that is one of Disgusto's teeth, it can't tell us where to find him."

Cube smiled. "It may do just that, if you allow yourself to think *outside* the box. Although, of course, I myself do all my thinking *inside* a box..." The professor began to giggle at his own bad joke.

"You're such a square," Fangs grumbled.

"Really?" said Cube. "Thank you very much!" He peered back through the eyepiece of the microscope. "You see this tooth has a most unusual filling."

"Unusual in what way?" I asked.

"Well, fillings are generally made from some kind of amalgam," Cube explained. "Mercury mixed with another material, such as silver, zinc or even copper. But this tooth is filled with concrete."

"Nonsense!" barked Fangs. "I've never heard of anyone having their cavities filled with concrete."

"Just because you haven't heard of it, doesn't mean it doesn't exist," retorted Cube. "This could be a very important lead."

"It could mean the owner of the tooth has to have their dental work done on the cheap," I suggested.

"Exactly." Cube beamed. "And to my knowledge – of which there is a considerable amount – there is only one dentist in the world who would perform that sort of shoddy, backstreet work. Nicolas Sizer."

"We've got our first lead!" I cried. "Sizer will be able to tell us whether or not this is the Great Disgusto's tooth. Do you know where we can find him, professor?"

"He's often hard to track down," he said.
"But I may have a couple of addresses for him,
somewhere in the *corner* of my mind..."

Fangs set the automatic pilot on the sleek
MP1 jet and then joined me in the cabin. We were
on our way to France after Cube had helped us to
track down Sizer's current address – 230 Rue de
Wakening, Paris.

"But why would Zed have one of the Great
Disgusto's teeth?" I asked.

"If that tooth *does* belong to Disgusto," Fangs
reminded me.

"We should know soon enough. Arrival in Paris expected in just under fifteen minutes," I said, looking at the GPS on my laptop.

Fangs settled back in his seat and closed his eyes. "Wake me up when we get there."

"No time to nap, Agent Enigma," barked a tinny voice. Cube's face appeared in a window on my laptop screen, fitting the space perfectly. "You'll find your latest selection of gadgets in the locker above you."

Fangs sighed and pulled a flight case down from the overhead compartment. "What have you lumbered us with this time?" he asked.

Cube beamed. "What you have in front of you are my very latest inventions – cutting-edge technology that will aid you in your quest to find and apprehend this magical miscreant Disgusto."

Fangs lifted a plastic kettle out of the case. "Cutting-edge?" he sneered.

"Don't be so quick to dismiss my work, Enigma. That particular gizmo took months to develop."

"But it's a kettle..."

"Not just any kettle," said Cube. "If you look inside, you'll find a high-tech tracking device hard-wired to the heating element."

Fangs lifted the lid and peered inside. "So it's a *tracking* kettle?"

"Precisely. Just plant it anywhere on the Great Disgusto's person, and Puppy will be able to use the GPS on her computer to follow him wherever he goes."

"You want us to hide a *kettle* somewhere on Disgusto?" Fangs asked.

Cube nodded. "Somewhere he won't discover it and become suspicious."

"If he does find it, I'm sure he'll think it's just one of the *many* kettles he carries round with him all the time," said Fangs sarcastically.

"Exactly," said Cube, missing the mocking tone

in my boss's voice completely. "He'll have no idea he's being tracked by MP1."

"Tracked by MP1 until he makes a cup of tea, that is," Fangs pointed out.

"What?"

"I'm presuming the tracking device is electrical."

"Of course," said Cube. "It's an electro-silicon compound of my own design—"

"That will survive being immersed in boiling water when the kettle is used?"

Cube blinked behind his square glasses and was silent for a moment. "Perhaps I'd better go back to square one with that particular item."

"Perhaps," Fangs agreed.

"Next," Cube said, moving on, "you'll find an emergency mode of transportation, should you need it."

"A skateboard," said Fangs, peering into the case.

"A *rocket-powered* skateboard," Cube corrected. "And, finally, I've provided you with a particularly interesting item of clothing."

I picked up a pair of underpants covered in pictures of bright-red chilli peppers. "You mean these?"

"I do indeed, Agent Brown," replied Cube. "The material has been infused with seeds from one of the hottest chilli plants in the world."

"Why on earth would you make a pair of chilli underpants?" Fangs asked.

Cube shrugged. "Because the banana ones kept running in the wash."

An alert sounded from the cockpit, and I glanced at the GPS on my laptop. "We're closing in on Paris, boss," I said. "And I think—"

"Not a moment too soon," Fangs interrupted. "Sorry to cut our jolly little chat short, Cube, but we've got an ugly wizard to find."

"Just don't cause any chaos, Enigma," Cube

warned. "The prime minister is in Paris today, giving a fascinating speech on—"

"*Kssssssssttttttt!*" Fangs made a hissing sound into the laptop microphone while waving his cape back and forth in front of the camera. "Sorry, Cube... *Kssssst...* We're losing you... *Kkkweeeeekkkk...* I think we're going through a tunnel... *Jzzzttt!*"

Cube scowled. "How can you be going through a tunnel? You're flying at over thirty thousand—"

Fangs clicked the "x" on the corner of the video feed, closing the connection. "That'll keep him quiet for a while." He grinned. "Now we can just sit back and relax until we're toasting croissants in the most romantic city in the world." He slumped back into one of the cabin's leather seats.

I looked past him through the cockpit window. "The croissants might not be the only things that are toasted," I said.

Fangs clasped his hands behind his head. "What do you mean?"

45

"You may want to think about some extra training on how to set the autopilot function of these jets."

"Extra training?" said Fangs indignantly, opening his eyes.

The Eiffel Tower was looming large through the cockpit window. After leaping out of his seat, Fangs lunged for the controls and pulled the plane's nose up just far enough to miss the top of the monument – and a group of terrified tourists – by a few centimetres.

After getting his breath back, Fangs turned to me and quipped, "Well, that gave them quite an *eye-ful*!"

I groaned.

An hour later, we were edging our way along Rue
de Wakening – a filthy backstreet in one of the
seedier districts of Paris. "This must be it," I said,
glancing up at the sign above the door. It was
in the shape of a tooth and looked appropriately
decayed. "What's the plan?"

"Leave it to me," Fangs said, baring his sharp vampire teeth. "I'll make sure he gets the *point*..."

Inside, the surgery was little more than a dingy apartment, and we found ourselves standing in the kitchen with a bored-looking receptionist. I guess she wasn't happy that Sizer liked to work so late. After we told her that Fangs was a tourist in need of an urgent filling, she sent us through to a living room that looked like it hadn't been cleaned in years. We sat in mismatched armchairs and flicked through the selection of magazines on the coffee table while we waited.

"This looks a little out of place," said Fangs, picking up a pristine copy of *Gold Trader* magazine from the stack of battered comics and old newspapers. "Not *exactly* the reading material of an incompetent dentist."

"Maybe one of his customers left it here?" I suggested.

"Next!" a voice called out.

"OK," said Fangs, standing up. "Let's get the truth about that tooth."

"I'll be with you in a moment, monsieur," said Nicolas Sizer without turning round as we entered what had once been the flat's only bedroom and was now Sizer's dental surgery.

Fangs settled back in the dentist's chair, which was next to a tray of equipment that had clearly seen better days. I waited near the door, in case our suspect tried to make a quick getaway once he realized who we were.

"Now," said Nicolas Sizer, choosing a rusted metal scaler and turning to my boss. "What have we got here?"

"You've got trouble!" snarled Fangs, flashing his MPl identification card.

The dentist's eyes widened. He snatched up a metal bowl and swung it at my boss's head. Fangs moved as quick as lightning, leaping to his feet and grabbing Sizer's wrist, just in time to stop the metallic dish colliding with his skull. Then he pushed Sizer into his own dentist's chair and plucked another scaler from the nearby tray. He brought the sharp tool in close to Sizer's teeth.

"Don't look so *down in the mouth*," Fangs growled. "We're only going to ask you some questions."

The trembling dentist nodded.

I pulled the mystery molar we had found on Zed from a pocket in my utility belt. "We know you worked on this tooth," I said. "We want to know who it belongs to."

"That could be anybody's tooth," spat Sizer.

"Well, we know it's not one of yours," said Fangs, jabbing at Sizer's teeth with the scaler. "Yours are all safely tucked away in here – for now." He gripped the dentist's cheeks harder. "Whose tooth is it?"

"I ... I can't tell you..." Sizer gurgled. "He'll k-kill me if I tell you!"

"Wrong answer!" Fangs barked, and he began to scratch his initials into Sizer's two front teeth. "You *can* tell us – at the moment... But that's all about to change." 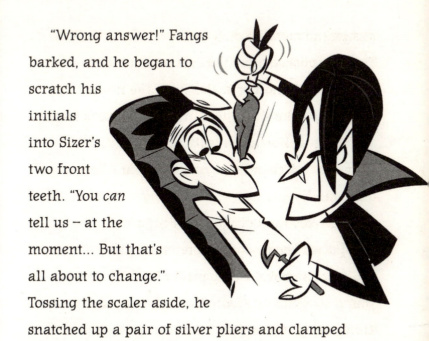 Tossing the scaler aside, he snatched up a pair of silver pliers and clamped them around the dentist's tongue.

"Nwo! Nwot my twongue!" sobbed Sizer. "Wou wouldn't!"

"He would," I said. "But he won't if you tell us about the tooth." I watched calmly as Fangs stretched Sizer's tongue out from between his teeth. I understand that my boss sometimes has to threaten villains to get the information he needs, but he only ever uses violence as a last resort. The bad guys don't know that, though, which is why they always crack.

"Th-the Great Disgusto," croaked Sizer. "It's one of the Great Disgusto's teeth."

Fangs released the dentist's tongue. "Very good," he said. "Now tell us why a rotting zombie would want to carry a tooth halfway around the world."

"I don't know what you're talking about."

Fangs threw me a wry glance. "And he was doing so well," he snarled, grabbing a drill this time and bringing it close to the dentist's mouth. The room was filled with a high-pitched whining sound.

"You know the *drill* by now," Fangs said. "Answer the question and your *brush* with us will be at an end."

"OK, OK," cried Sizer. "Don't hurt me! Disgusto wanted to know h-how much his teeth would be worth on the b-black market."

"The Great Disgusto wanted to sell his teeth?" said Fangs.

Sizer nodded. "But only before he accidentally ... accidentally..." The dentist slumped to one side, consciousness draining away.

"Fangs!" I shouted, pointing to an air vent in the wall behind the chair. Plumes of thick, green gas were flowing through the metal grille and slowly but surely filling the room. The stuff smelled like a skunk that hadn't changed its socks in a month. Within seconds we were completely enveloped, and Nicolas Sizer was out cold.

"Get him out," Fangs ordered, his cape pressed to his mouth. "I'll let in some air."

As I dragged the unconscious dentist out of the chair, Fangs hurled the trolley of tools at the window. The glass smashed, and a weak breeze filtered into the room. It did little to disperse the thick gas.

I dumped Sizer on the carpet in the waiting room. "He's safe, boss," I called back into the gloom. "You need to get out of there. You don't want to—"

THUMP!

I grabbed a magazine from the coffee table and wafted enough of the gas away to spot Fangs lying unconscious on the surgery floor.

"—pass out." I sighed. After taking a deep breath of clean air, I plunged back into the stinking green cloud.

Fangs came round about twenty minutes later. He was lying on the couch in the waiting room with his cape wrapped around him like a blanket. "Wassah?" he slurred. "I sorra wissa gas..."

"It's OK," I assured him. "The gas has all gone now. I opened all the windows once I'd got you and Sizer to safety."

Fangs sat bolt upright – the name of our suspect obviously reminding him of the events of the past half-hour. "Where is Sizer?" he asked.

"I let him go."

Fangs's pale cheeks flushed ... well, they were a little less pale for a moment. "You let him go? Did breathing in that gas turn you insane?"

"Don't worry," I said. "I made him a cup of tea first."

I've never seen my boss's eyes grow so wide. "Tea?!" he roared. "Oh, that's just wonderful. I do hope you gave him a couple of biscuits to go with his cuppa."

"Calm down, boss. I made him a cup of tea with our kettle – the one with the homing device inside."

"So?"

"So ... you were right about that homing chip melting down when heated. As soon as the kettle boiled, the chip inside dissolved – and Sizer drank

55

the whole thing with his tea." I spun my laptop round so Fangs could see the green dot blinking on my GPS tracking system.

Fangs peered at the screen for a second, then his eyes flicked back up at me. "The homing device is still working – and we can track Sizer wherever he goes?"

"To within thirty centimetres."

"And he's bound to run straight to Disgusto to warn him we're on his trail..."

"Exactly."

Fangs beamed. "That's brilliant."

I blushed beneath my fur. "Thank you, boss."

"Brilliant of *me* to point out that the tracking device would melt once the kettle was used and so giving you the idea."

I smiled. "Yes, it was brilliant of you. Well done, sir."

Fangs pulled his sunglasses from his pocket and slipped them on. "All in a day's work, Brown.

Now where's our dastardly dentist headed?"

The green dot was moving quickly along the streets of the French capital on the map open on my laptop screen. After a few moments, it stopped.

Fangs squinted at the screen. "What's happening?"

"It looks like Sizer's gone inside somewhere."

A few mouse clicks later, and I had access to one of the nearby traffic cameras. I zoomed in on a brass plaque above the door of a large building.

"It's the British Embassy," I gasped.

Fangs arched an eyebrow. "If Sizer has run to tell Disgusto we're on his trail, then Disgusto must be at the embassy too."

"I don't like it," I said. "An embassy is a government building, just as the German Consulate is, which is where everyone was robbed last week."

"The robbery Phlem was certain Disgusto had committed."

"Exactly," I said.

"So let's get to the embassy and stop him."

"We'll have to be careful, boss. The prime minister's there tonight, giving a speech, remember. Phlem will go mad if we charge in, causing trouble."

Fangs smiled. "Phlem won't know anything about it. Not if we go in disguise..."

The word "disguise" turned out to be a little too grand a term for the way Fangs and I ended up dressed.

After arriving at the British Embassy, we skirted round to the back of the building, where we found two waiters taking a break outside an open door to the kitchen.

"Right," Fangs hissed. "I'll give them the old karate chop to the back of the neck to knock them out and then we'll drag them behind the bins and steal their clothes."

A few minutes later, we were climbing into the uniforms of the now unconscious waiters. There was one problem, though... The uniforms were both much too large.

"This never happens in movies," I muttered as I tightened my utility belt around trousers that were at least three sizes too big. "We look like a pair of clowns."

So, uniforms hanging off us, Fangs and I each collected a tray of drinks from the serving hatch in the kitchen and stepped out into the banqueting suite. The sight of it took my breath away.

It was the size of a football pitch. I'd been to towns that were smaller than this room. Huge stone pillars stretched up to a glass-domed ceiling and dozens of beautifully laid tables covered a thick carpet. Smartly dressed waiters and waitresses sailed from table to table, offering a choice of drinks to guests that included the richest, most influential people in the world. Politicians passed the time with princes, landowners laughed with lords, and businessmen bantered with barons. Everyone here was important and wealthy, and if the Great Disgusto was here too, that could only mean trouble. We had to find him, and fast.

I scanned the room. I could see no sign of Disgusto or Nicolas Sizer, but I did spy the British prime minister, Sir Hugh Jands, stepping up to a microphone that had been set up on a small stage. After glancing at a sheaf of notes in his hand, he ran a finger through his bushy moustache and then coughed politely. The noise echoed through the sound system.

The chatter in the banqueting hall subsided – and that's when I saw it. Snaking out from behind the stage was a thin wisp of green smoke. It had to be the same gas that had knocked out Sizer and Fangs at the surgery – and now it was about to flood into the British Embassy!

"Ladies and gentlemen, *mesdames et monsieurs...*" began the prime minister, oblivious to the green smoke that was now wafting around his polished shoes.

I tapped one of my front teeth with my tongue. I knew the tooth would be glowing blue as the radio link activated. "Fangs," I hissed. "Look at the stage."

Fangs didn't reply. I looked around and spotted him serving a drink to a young woman in a red dress on the other side of the room. "Fangs," I said again, but he gave no indication that he had heard me.

The prime minister, now ankle-deep in emerald-coloured fumes, was continuing his speech. "...It gives me great pleasure to welcome you all here tonight for what I trust will be an evening to remember."

"Fangs!" I barked. We had to evacuate the place before everybody fell victim to the gas. I clamped my paws over my ears to block out the background noise and tried to make out what Fangs was saying through our two-way radio. I didn't like what I heard...

"The name's Enigma," he said. "Fangs Enigma."

Surely he wasn't going to do this now.

"...Perhaps after Sir Hugh has finished his speech, we could take a stroll along the banks of the River Seine?"

He *was* going to do this now!

I raced over and prodded him. "Boss, I think we should keep our minds on the job."

He glared down at me. "I have got my mind on the job, Brown," he hissed. "I'm busy interrogating a suspect."

I glanced at the young woman standing before us. She had thick red hair, porcelain-white

skin and big green eyes. Huge diamond earrings dangled from her ears, and she was clutching a scarlet handbag that matched her dress, lipstick and perfectly manicured fingernails.

"Hi," she said in a thick, deep Southern drawl. "My name's Milly. Milly O'Naire. Your friend here was just telling me about the banks of the River Seine. Do you think one of those banks will have a cashpoint machine? I'm a little short of spending money."

"Don't you worry your pretty little head about money," Fangs said. "I can open you a cuddle account for free."

I almost screamed with frustration. Everyone – from the prime minister down – was about to be gassed, and my boss was busy chatting up a girl! It looked like saving them all was going to be up to me.

Dumping my tray of drinks, I raced for the stage, planning on grabbing Sir Hugh and dragging him away to safety when—

65

CRASH!

Something small, hard and covered in jewellery attacked me from the right and sent me hurtling into a nearby table. A tiny, grey figure landed on my chest as I fell. It gnashed at me with its sharp teeth while raining down blows with its miniature fists. It was a gnome. A gnome wearing a designer tracksuit and a backwards baseball cap. After grabbing the creature by its collar, I held it at arm's length.

"Yo, yo!" it cried angrily. *"My name is Hip Hop. I'm the master of rhyme. The master of crime. Don't you waste my time!"*

Then he began to make a noise like a beat box. *"Ba-bum-bum-chi, bum-bum-chi. Ba-bum-bum-chi, fwee-hee, fwee-hee, fwee-hee, fwee!"*

I was beginning to wonder whether I'd hit my head on the table as I'd fallen, when I heard a crash from the stage. Sir Hugh Jands was stumbling around, trying to waft the green gas away, and he'd knocked over his microphone. There was no way I could get him and everyone else out before they started to fall unconscious. I had to find a way to block the air vent – but how?

"Yo, yo!" rapped the gnome. "Don't mess wit' me. I'll bust yo' face. Make you a disgrace. A waste of space!"

The gnome! Of course. I leapt up onto the stage, then ran past the prime minister and slammed Hip Hop against the air vent, using his body to cut off as much of the gas as I could. He only covered about three quarters of the vent, and thin tendrils of green still leaked out, but it was the best I could do.

The gnome struggled furiously.

"Yo, yo!" he shouted. "Let me go. Now this ain't cool. I ain't no tool. Release me, fool!"

"Oh, shut up!" I said, snatching the gnome's baseball hat from his head and stuffing it into his mouth.

I spotted something glinting in the darkness of the air vent beyond Hip Hop. Something that glinted like gold. I grabbed my night-vision goggles from my utility belt, pushed Hip Hop's head to one side and peered into the gloom.

Staring back at me was the ugly face of the Great Disgusto.

"**Fangs!**" I yelled into my blue tooth.

"I've found Disgusto, and I'm going after him!"
Without waiting for a reply, I dropped the gnome
and wrenched the cover off the air vent. It was
a squeeze to get in, but the metal tunnel then
widened out enough for me to crawl inside it on
my hands and knees.

Luckily, the flow of pungent gas seemed to have stopped. Cool air rushed past me thanks to the air-conditioning system. It blew away the remaining fumes, allowing me to see better. I doubted it would be strong enough to clear the entire banqueting hall, however. It would be up to Fangs to save the people there.

Up ahead, the Great Disgusto was crawling away from me as fast as his hands and knees could carry him. He turned a corner in the pipe and disappeared.

"Disgusto!" I shouted, making the turn myself. "This is Agent Brown of MP1. You are wanted for questioning in relation to—" Something was pulling me back. I looked over my shoulder, afraid that Hip Hop had crawled into the air duct after me, but the gnome wasn't the problem. My waiter's trousers had caught on a loose screw jutting out of the tunnel wall.

I tried to free myself, but I couldn't reach the

screw and the tunnel was too narrow for me to turn round and unhook the trousers by hand. I jerked my leg from side to side in an effort to rip the material.

"Well, well, Agent Brown," said a voice behind me. "It appears that you are trapped."

The Great Disgusto had backed up in the tunnel and was gazing over his shoulder at me. Luckily, his body was in the way, so I couldn't see much of his hideous face.

"You've made a big mistake, Disgusto," I growled. "As soon as I'm free, you'll be coming in for questioning."

"No," said the Great Disgusto quietly, "I won't."

What he did next was the last thing I would ever have expected an internationally wanted villain to do. He pulled down his trousers to reveal a gleaming golden bottom – and he farted in my face.

Stinking green gas – the same gas that had filled the dentist's surgery and the banqueting hall – flooded the air-conditioning tunnel. Then everything went black.

I came round about an hour later. Disgusto was, of course, nowhere to be seen. Groggily, I kicked my leg, ripping my trousers free from the screw. Then I edged back along the tunnel until I reached the banqueting hall.

It was total chaos. Everyone in the room – guests and waiters alike – had been gassed. They were all slowly starting to regain consciousness, woozily sitting up as though they had woken from the deepest sleep of their lives.

I found Fangs lying face down in a large salad on one of the buffet tables. "Come on, boss," I said, helping him to his feet and pulling a stick of celery out of one of his nostrils. "How are you feeling?"

"Like I've had a hard night on blood milkshakes." Fangs groaned, clutching his forehead. He began to pat his pockets. "Where are my sunglasses?"

"Never mind that," croaked a man at the next table. "My wallet's gone!"

"And my necklace!" cried a woman. "All my jewellery's missing."

One by one, people discovered that all their belongings had been taken. From tiaras to the waiters' wages – everything was gone.

Disgusto either hadn't thought to rob me or hadn't had time because I still had my utility belt and mobile phone. "I think we'd better call the police," I said, and then I told Fangs what had happened in the tunnel.

Within half an hour, uniformed officers had arrived and were taking statements from the

guests and waiting staff. "This is a waste of time,"
grumbled Fangs. "We should be out there, looking
for Disgusto. He might know where my sunglasses
have gone."

"And everyone else's belongings," I reminded
him. I was busy trying to hack into the embassy's
security network on my laptop.

"Yes, of course," agreed Fangs
quickly. "All that other stuff too."
Once inside the network,
I played back the footage
from the closed-circuit
television cameras
inside the banqueting suite.

A crisp black-and-white image sprang to life, and
I smiled.

"Got them!" I said.

The recording showed the Great Disgusto,
Nicolas Sizer and Hip Hop walking among the
unconscious figures of the embassy's guests and

74

waiters. Each of them wore a gas mask to protect them from the remnants of the noxious fumes. Fangs and I watched the trio remove wallets from people's pockets, unclasp necklaces from throats and pull rings from fingers. At one point, Disgusto turned towards the camera, revealing a pair of dark glasses over his eyes.

"My sunglasses!" exclaimed Fangs. "That gas must be powerful stuff if he was able to take those from me without a fight."

"It's very powerful," I agreed. "I just can't believe it came from Disgusto's bum."

"And you say his bottom was gold?" Fangs said.

I nodded. The image of the golden behind was burned into my memory. I was sure I'd never forget it.

"Was it painted gold? Was he wearing some sort of artificial buttocks?"

"I don't know. I only got a quick glance before he used it on me."

"And it farted out the same gas we saw at the dentist surgery?"

"Exactly the same – which means Disgusto was already at the surgery when we arrived. I thought the gas attack there was a little convenient."

But Fangs wasn't listening. Milly O'Naire had finished giving her statement to the police and was heading our way.

"Puppy!" Fangs cried. "Tell the police to arrest Miss Milly O'Naire."

Milly froze, her eyes widening with horror. "What? Why?"

Fangs's lips curled up into a smile. "Because it must be illegal to look that beautiful. Maybe I could take you to dinner and question you further?"

Milly smiled and ran her fingers through her hair, making her diamond earrings sparkle in the light. "I'm afraid I'm late for another appointment."

She opened her red purse and produced a business card. "Why don't you give me a call sometime?" She raised herself up onto her toes and kissed my boss on the cheek, before striding, hips wiggling, from the room.

Fangs leaned back to watch her go, accidentally resting his hand on a tray of nibbles instead of the table. The tray flipped up, showering his face with food. A prawn hung from his right ear like a bright pink earring.

Like an earring! I'd almost missed a vital clue.

"You were right!" I exclaimed. "We should have got the police to arrest her. Milly O'Naire is in league with the Great Disgusto."

"What are you talking about?" Fangs asked.

"She was still wearing her earrings. And she opened her *purse* to hand you her card."

"So?"

77

"So Milly O'Naire is the only person in this room who wasn't robbed. We've got to stop her." I ran towards the main entrance of the embassy, skidding through the marbled entrance hall and leaping down the steps that led out onto the street – but I was too late.

Milly O'Naire had disappeared.

Fangs spun the wheel of the sports car and
skidded onto Avenue des Champs-Élysées, the
needle on the speedometer twitching at just below
a hundred kilometres per hour. "Any sign of her?"
he asked.

"Not yet," I replied, scanning the crowds of tourists through my binoculars. "But we have to find her. Disgusto, Sizer and Hip Hop disappeared long before we regained consciousness. Milly's our only link to them."

"Then we'll keep looking," said Fangs, swerving to avoid a cyclist. He mounted the roundabout in the centre of the road and took a short cut beneath the Arc de Triomphe.

As far as we knew, Milly O'Naire was travelling on foot, or at best had hailed a taxi cab. We, on the other hand, had access to one of twelve high-powered motor vehicles that MP1 kept parked in key locations all over Paris – just as they did in all the major cities of the world. All Fangs had had to do was press his thumb against the sensor on the door lock, and we had transport.

"You gave her your real name," I said to Fangs. "Do you think she knows who you are?"

Fangs shook his head. "I don't think so. She just gave me her card and asked me to call."

"Her card!" I exclaimed. "Can I look at it?"

Fangs handed over the lightly scented business card.

"Perfect," I said. "It's got her phone number on it."

"Don't you think it might give away the fact that we're following her if you call to ask where she's going?"

I flipped open my laptop. "I'm not going to call her. I can track the position of her mobile phone via the GPS software." I launched the program, linked up to the several communications satellites orbiting above us and then tapped in Milly's number. Almost instantly, a green dot began to flash on the screen. I dragged a digital map of Paris over the image to get a precise location.

"She's moving fast," I said, watching as the dot

whizzed along a main street. "She must be in a taxi after all."

"Where's she headed?"

"The airport, I'd say. She must be catching a plane somewhere."

"Then let's fly..." Fangs spun the car 180 degrees and roared away towards the airport, tyres squealing.

My boss levelled the jet out at cruising height. "I've always liked the south of France at this time of year," he said.

Before we'd taken off, I'd hacked into the airport's passenger records for that day's travel. Miss Milly O'Naire had booked onto flight AF2811 to Nice, with an additional helicopter ride on to Monaco.

"Are you sure Milly didn't recognize your name? We don't want to walk into a trap."

"It's a risk we'll have to take," said Fangs, setting the autopilot – and making sure he got it right this time. "Are you still tracking her phone?"

I shook my head. "She switched it off when she boarded her plane, but I managed to download everything in its memory before she did. And I found this." I moved the mouse over my laptop screen to a file named TO BE SENT TO EVERY GOVERNMENT IN THE WORLD! and double clicked. Shaky footage began to play. It had clearly been recorded on the phone's camera. A familiar figure stepped into view.

"The Great Disgusto!" exclaimed Fangs.

As we watched, the Great Disgusto turned to the camera. "Are you filming now?" he asked.

"Of course I am," snapped the voice of Milly O'Naire.

"All right," said Disgusto, smoothing down his tattered wizard's robes. He then addressed the camera directly. "Governments of the world – pay close attention. Laid out before me, you will see the ingredients for my latest invention." The camera panned down to reveal a bowl of brownish powder with a fuse wire coming out of it. "I have discovered a rare compound that, when mixed with wizard DNA at high temperatures, will produce pure gold."

"That's ... incredible." Milly gasped, off-screen.

"It is, indeed." Disgusto beamed. "I shall use this powder to turn all of my teeth gold, and I will then have them removed to sell on the black market..."

"That explains why he's been hanging around with a backstreet dentist like Nicolas Sizer," Fangs said.

"And why we found a gold-trading magazine in Sizer's waiting room," I added.

The Great Disgusto was still raving at the camera. "...But I don't just want to be rich. I want to be filthy, stinking rich! I want to have more money than I know what to do with. And so, with the profits from selling my teeth, I shall buy a missile to fire at one of your parliament buildings. But only after you EACH pay me a million dollars will I reveal which government is the target. That government may then attempt to bribe me into changing my mind. I can't lose!"

Milly zoomed in as the Great Disgusto lit the fuse that led to the bowl of powder. He bent forward and bared his teeth. The fuse burned shorter and shorter, the sparking flame scorching the tabletop as it rushed towards the powder.

Disgusto closed his eyes. His whole body was trembling as he pulled his lips back from his teeth with his fingers...

Then the doorbell to his laboratory rang.

The Great Disgusto spun round angrily. "Who on earth is that at this time of—"

KABOOM!

The flash powder exploded, showering Disgusto's bottom in a fine, glittery mist.

Disgusto screamed and hopped around the lab, clutching his burned behind. I notched up the volume on the laptop. Milly was giggling behind the camera.

"That was the last of my powder!" shouted the Great Disgusto. "I can't afford any more! How can I sell my teeth if they aren't made of gold? How can I buy a missile if I can't sell my teeth?" He slumped down onto a stool and a metallic *CLANG!* rang out.

At the sound, Disgusto stood up again slowly and unfastened his trousers. He turned round. As he pulled the waistband down at the back, Fangs and I got a glimpse of a golden buttock. Milly O'Naire screamed, and the video cut off.

"So his bottom *is* solid gold," said Fangs.

"Although that still doesn't explain how he can gas people with it."

The GPS software began to beep. "We're almost in Monaco," I said.

"We'd better get changed into something more suitable," Fangs said. He was right. There was no way we'd be able to mingle with the rich and famous of the French Riviera dressed like this.

I closed my laptop and unclipped my utility belt – and something soft fell onto my foot. It was a tiny baseball cap. "Hip Hop's hat," I said, picking it up. "It must have got caught in my belt when I threw him aside to chase the Great Disgusto.

"Not much use to us now," said Fangs. "Unless we have to dress some dolls as part of this case."

"I suppose not," I agreed. "Wait. The lining of the cap's all sticky – like it's covered in honey."

Fangs smiled. "Sounds like you've made a *beeline* to another clue!"

Fangs pulled the MP1 stretch limo up to the front of the casino and handed the keys to the parking attendant with the order: "Replenish the milk bar!"

We mounted the casino steps, looking every bit like wealthy gamblers. Fangs wore a tuxedo and I was in a black, sequined dress.

"I found out what that sticky substance was on Hip Hop's cap," I whispered.

"Honey?" asked Fangs.

"It wasn't honey. It was sap. Sap from *Jatropha curcas*, a plant that grows in the Philippines. It's also known as the tuba-tuba plant and it's incredibly toxic."

"So what was Hip Hop doing with it?"

"Beats me. Coupled with the mushroom grains we found on Zed, it's got the capacity to make someone very ill indeed."

"The question," said Fangs, "is who?"

A casino manager, wearing a blazer with the company logo on the breast pocket, stepped forward to greet us. "Good evening, Monsieur Enigma, Mademoiselle Brown – your table is waiting. Please come this way."

"We're expected," I hissed. "Milly must have known who you are. The business card *was* a trap after all."

"Let's see what else is waiting for us," said Fangs with a snarl.

We followed the manager through the bustling casino, past slot machines and roulette wheels, until we reached a card table covered in baize. Two further employees held chairs out for us, and a barmaid placed drinks in front of us: a blood milkshake for Fangs and an orange juice for me.

"This is all very pleasant." Fangs smiled.

"Don't speak too soon," I said. Approaching the table were the Great Disgusto and Milly O'Naire.

"Agent Enigma," said Disgusto. "So pleased you could join us. I knew you wouldn't be able to resist following my little clue." He pulled Milly's chair out for her and then sat down himself, his bottom making a faint metallic *Ding!*

Milly looked gorgeous in a stunning white dress. I crossed my claws in the hope that Fangs would be able to stay focused.

The barmaid reappeared, with a glass of champagne for Milly, and a bottle of milk and a glass for the Great Disgusto. Fangs licked his lips at the sight of the white liquid. "A man with good taste, I see," he said.

"I doubt very much whether this would be your kind of tipple," said Disgusto, opening the bottle. A foul stench wafted across the table. The milk was off! Rancid lumps of the stuff slopped into the glass as the wizard poured it out.

"That milk may be slightly past its sell-by date," Fangs suggested.

"The further past it, the better!" Disgusto reached into his jacket pocket and produced two silver boxes. From the first, he sprinkled small brown granules into the sour milk.

"Tigertop mushroom!" I gasped.

"I see you've done your homework, Miss Brown," said the Great Disgusto with a smile. "Then you should also have worked out that this

93

box contains tuba-tuba sap." He drizzled a little of the sticky liquid into his drink and then stirred it all together. The mixture turned dark green and began to fizz.

"I presume you're not here to display your cocktail-making skills," said Fangs.

"Oh no," said Disgusto. "My stomach agitator is just a guilty pleasure. We are here to play!" He downed his drink in one go. "What do you say, Enigma? Shall we make this game a little more ... interesting?"

"In what way?"

"A little wager, perhaps?" The Great Disgusto reached inside his jacket pocket again and this time pulled out two diamond earrings and a pair of sunglasses.

"Those are mine!" growled Fangs. "The sunglasses, I mean – not the earrings."

"The earrings match the description of those stolen from the prime minister's wife at the British Embassy," I said.

"Finders keepers..." teased Disgusto.

"I'd rather play for information," snarled Fangs. "How about you tell us of your plans to blow up a parliament building."

A smile spread across Disgusto's foul face. "You've watched my video? All right. If you win our little game, I'll tell you everything."

Fangs remained stern. *"And give me back my sunglasses?"*

"Of course! But what if I win? What are you putting down as your stake?"

My boss nodded at me. MPI provides all its agents with a large amount of spending money for use in situations like this. I opened my purse and laid a thick wodge of banknotes on the table. "Is three thousand euros enough?"

Disgusto nodded. "Let's play..."

Milly kissed him on the cheek.
"Good luck, honey."

"I don't need luck," the Great
Disgusto said as a casino employee
began to deal out the cards. "This is a game of
skill and tactics, and I'm a world master."

He picked up his cards and studied them.
His face was set like stone and his eyes revealed
no emotion at all. Eventually, he chose a card and
placed it face up on the table. It featured a picture
of a round, jolly woman wearing an apron and
carrying a rolling pin. "Do you have Mr Bun
the baker?"

Fangs glanced down at his own cards. "No."

The corner of Disgusto's mouth twitched.

My boss pulled out a card from his hand and
slapped it down on the table. It showed a little boy
lying back in a chair with his mouth wide open.
"Do you have Mr Drill the dentist?"

The Great Disgusto's face split into a wide grin.

"I'm afraid not, Agent Enigma. Our dentist friend, Mr Sizer, proved to be too much trouble and should right about now be parachuting into the darkest jungle in all of Peru."

Milly O'Naire giggled.

"But let's not let that spoil our evening," continued Disgusto. He played a card with a picture of a man holding up a large glittering ruby. "Do you have Mrs Gem the jeweller's wife?"

"I'm afraid not," Fangs said. "But I do have Mr Cuffs the policeman." He tossed the card down onto the green baize.

"Curses!" growled Disgusto. He hurled one of his own cards down on top of the policeman. On it was a picture of a young boy blowing a whistle and wielding a truncheon.

"Why, thank you," said Fangs, sliding the card over to his side of the table. "I have a feeling you'll be seeing the rest of the policeman's family very soon."

97

"I wouldn't bet on it," Disgusto said. "In fact, as soon as— Argh!" He doubled over, clutching his stomach.

"I see the pressure of the game is getting to you," said Fangs.

The Great Disgusto raised his head, a twisted expression of pain etched across his already hideous face. "Oh, this isn't pressure. This just means my stomach agitator is ready to roll. Milly!"

At his command, Milly snatched up the earrings, money and sunglasses from the table. Disgusto, meanwhile, had dropped his trousers and spun round so his golden bottom was pointed straight at us.

But, this time, we were ready. Fangs and I each pulled out a gas mask. We were about to strap them over our faces when were grabbed from behind. The croupier had a tight grip on Fangs while my arms were pinned behind my back by the cocktail waitress. But that wasn't the biggest surprise.

Everyone else in the casino – gamblers, card dealers, bar staff, even the manager – was wearing a gas mask.

"They can't *all* be working for you," I said to Disgusto.

"Of course not," the Great Disgusto said as he and Milly pulled on gas masks of their own. "I simply promised to pay them handsomely if they all played along."

"Well, it's the only way the word *handsome* could be used around you," said Fangs.

Disgusto's smile fell away. "Good night, Agent Enigma," he growled.

FART!

* * *

I came round to find myself dangling in the air. My arms and legs had been tied together and I was in total darkness. This was not good news.

I used my sensitive werewolf hearing to try and pick up clues as to where I was. I could hear people talking, their voices muffled. Then there was another sound. One I recognized. The *clack, clack, clack* of a tiny silver ball bouncing around a spinning roulette wheel. That meant I was still somewhere inside the casino.

Something moved beside me and I stiffened – until I heard a familiar groan. I tapped my blue tooth with my tongue and hissed into the tiny microphone embedded inside. "Fangs? Is that you?"

"It's me. Where are we?"

Before I could reply, the room lit up. "I'll tell you exactly where you are, Agent Enigma," barked a voice from below. "You are in my clutches!"

100

I looked down. The Great Disgusto and Milly O'Naire were standing below us at the edge of a pool of water, and Fangs and I were dangling right above it!

"Disgusto!" snarled Fangs.

"How delightful to see you again, Agent Enigma."

"Well, we decided to *hang* around for a while," Fangs quipped.

"Why not?" said the wizard. "Monte Carlo suits you. I can see you both making a big *splash* here."

102

We eyed the pool beneath us. Something was swimming around in it. "What's in the water?" I asked.

"Piranha fish!" Disgusto announced with glee, pulling a raw chicken leg from his trouser pocket and dropping it into the pool. Instantly, the surface of the water was churned into froth as the hungry piranhas fought to devour the treat. Within seconds, the water had calmed again, and a piece of pure white bone floated to the surface.

"Enthusiastic little chaps, aren't they?" said Disgusto. "Such a shame Milly and I won't be here to watch you meet them." He strode over to where the rope holding us up in the air was tied to a metal hook in the wall. Below the rope was a wooden crate, on which was sat a single candle. As we watched, the Great Disgusto struck a match and lit the candle.

"The flame will burn slowly through the rope, eventually dropping the pair of you – still tied

103

up – into the piranha-infested pool," Disgusto said. "The water isn't very deep, so I imagine you'll hurt yourself quite badly in the fall, although that shouldn't be a problem for very long."

The candle flame flickered against the rope, sending up a thin stream of smoke. The rope was starting to burn already. Satisfied his plan was working, Disgusto took Milly's hand in his and walked to the door.

"Wait!" shouted Fangs. "I won the card game."

The Great Disgusto turned. "So?"

"You owe me information," said Fangs.

There was a faint *PING!* as the first few threads of rope burned away. Fangs and I dropped a centimetre or two closer to the deadly water below.

"I suppose that's fair," said Disgusto.

"Careful, honey," warned Milly. "Don't tell them your idea."

"Why not?" The wizard laughed. "They'll be dead in ten minutes."

PING!

Another few strands of the rope burned away, and we dropped another couple of centimetres. I hoped my boss knew what he was doing.

"After failing to turn my teeth gold, I could no longer sell them to raise money to buy my missile. I needed a new plan... Luckily, my golden bum provided the perfect one. With the money I'm stealing now, I can afford to buy enough missiles to threaten *every* parliament in the world. Then I can raise the ransom to a BILLION dollars per government!"

"Quite the retirement package," I said.

"Silence!" yelled Disgusto, his voice echoing off the bare walls of the storeroom. "Don't make me fart on the candle flame and hasten your inevitable demise."

"That's another thing," said Fangs calmly –

even though another *PING!* rang out and we dropped a little closer to our doom. "How *do* you knock people out with your bum?"

"That was my fault." Milly O'Naire giggled. "After my darling turned his butt to gold, he felt rather unwell, so I went to make him a health shake..."

Disgusto grinned. "The poor dear took ingredients from my spell cupboard by mistake. I really shouldn't have kept my magical supplies in the kitchen – although now I'm glad I did. You see, Milly accidentally stumbled upon the ingredients that, when combined and distilled through my golden bottom, produce a knockout gas."

"I spent the best part of three days unconscious," said Milly.

"And then Disgusto sent Zed and his other henchmen to buy up extra supplies of tigertop mushroom and tuba-tuba sap," I said to Fangs. "Of course!"

Another *PING!* The rope had burned almost all of the way through. Our heads were very nearly touching the water.

"Well, I can *see* we're keeping you from your grisly deaths, so we'll bid you a final farewell," said Disgusto. He led Milly out of the storeroom and closed the door.

I glanced down at the piranhas below us. "What are we going to do?"

"We're going to catch them," said Fangs, nodding at the door the Great Disgusto and Milly had just walked though. "Copy me!" Then he swung his body out as far as he could. I did the same, and slowly we began to swing from side to side.

PING!

I suddenly realized what Fangs had been doing. "You kept them talking while the rope burned through!" I exclaimed.

"Exactly," said Fangs. "Not only did Disgusto reveal his *stinker* of a plan, but he and Milly won't be too far away by the time we get out of this."

We continued to move our bodies, swinging wider and wider with each thrust.

"Now we know why Disgusto was at the dentist's surgery when we arrived there," I said. "He was trying to get his tooth back in case it fell into the wrong hands. But Nicolas Sizer had already given it to Zed."

"But why?" asked Fangs. "Why would Sizer give Disgusto's tooth to a zombie?"

"My guess is that Disgusto wanted to know how much his teeth would be worth on the black market after he'd turned them to gold – so he told Sizer to give the tooth to Zed to find out. But by the time Zed had got to Turkey, the plan had changed. Disgusto had turned his bum gold and learned about the stomach agitator, so he must have asked Zed to pick up the mushrooms instead."

PING!

We were swinging almost from wall to wall now, and there wasn't much left of the rope above the candle. We just had to hope that when it finally gave way, we weren't directly over the—

SNAP!

Fangs and I plummeted. We landed with a thump just centimetres from the edge of the pool. I used my sharp werewolf claws to cut through the ropes that still bound us.

Fangs smiled at the piranha fish. "So sorry not to be joining you for dinner."

We ran for the door and then followed the corridor as it led us through the casino kitchens and out into the cool night air. We were just in time to see the Great Disgusto and Milly roaring away on a motorbike.

"Get to the limo!" barked Fangs – but when we got to the car we saw that the tyres had been slashed.

"How far away is the nearest MPl garage?" Fangs asked.

"Too far," I replied.

"Then we've lost them!"

"Not necessarily." After opening the boot of the car, I pulled out the rocket-powered skateboard that Cube had given us.

"You've got to be kidding," said Fangs.

"We don't have an option. Now get on!"

There's a reason why the streets of Monaco are used for the annual Formula One Grand Prix race — the corners are tight, the straight sections are short and there's danger waiting at every turn. I would imagine, however, that the course is infinitely more comfortable and a lot safer behind the wheel of a racing car than it is on a bit of wood with four tiny wheels and an engine fuelled by the same stuff they use for space missions.

I clung onto Fangs as tightly as I could as he leaned left, then right, then left again, weaving between cars and dodging pedestrians. "I can see them up ahead," he shouted.

"Can we catch them?"

"I think so. They're heading out of the city, so they'll have to slow down to navigate the narrow mountain roads."

"Are we going to slow down as well?"

"Not a chance!"

The road began to rise as we left the town, but the skateboard's rocket engine made easy work of the climb. Before long, we were chasing the Great Disgusto along moonlit roads with a cliff-face on one side and a sheer drop on the other.

We were steadily gaining on them. I could see Milly's red hair billowing out behind her in the wind and hear Disgusto's curses as he watched our progress in his mirror.

Eventually, we pulled alongside the motorbike. "Disgusto!" Fangs yelled, his voice barely carrying over the noise of the two engines. "I'm placing you under arrest for—"

Disgusto punched Fangs square in the jaw, causing the skateboard to swerve violently towards the deadly drop beyond the road.

Fangs was forced to take evasive action and, leaning hard to his left, he took us along a smaller unpaved path that rose parallel to the main track. My teeth juddered as the rocket motor powered us over the uneven ground. This must have been the original mountain pass before the level of traffic became too heavy for it. Looking down, I could see Disgusto and Milly speeding along the newer road below.

"Hold on tight!" called Fangs. "I've got an idea."

Ahead of us were the ruins of an old wooden bridge. The entire middle section of it had fallen away. "You're not thinking of—"

"I sure am, Puppy!"

I screwed my eyes shut just as we blasted up onto the bridge and shot out into empty air. Everything seemed to move in slow motion as we sailed through the moonlight, spinning head over heels.

We landed, skateboard wheels clattering, on the far side of the bridge and, turning hard right, found ourselves back on the new road. In front of us was a single headlight. We had landed in front of the motorbike – and we were hurtling straight towards it! The Great Disgusto pulled my boss's sunglasses from his pocket and put them on. He was ready for this deadly game of chicken.

The gap between us shrank and the motorbike's headlight grew larger as we continued on our collision course.

Then, at the last moment, Disgusto jerked the motorbike to one side. As he shot past on our right, Fangs whipped out a hand to snatch the sunglasses from Disgusto's face. He missed, and his fingers became entangled in Milly O'Naire's flaming red hair instead.

She was pulled off the back of the motorbike and crashed onto the grassy bank at the side of the road. Fangs, his fingers still wrapped in her tresses, was pulled off balance, and both he and I tumbled from the skateboard. The board flew out from beneath us and rocketed off the side of the mountain, the flames from its engine lighting up the night sky as it exploded.

The tail-light of Disgusto's motorbike disappeared round a bend. I howled with frustration.

"Are you OK?" asked Fangs.

I nodded. "Just annoyed that we let the Great Disgusto escape!"

"We'll find him," Fangs assured me, pulling Milly to her feet. "Miss O'Naire is going to tell us exactly where he's going."

"I won't tell you a thing!" she spat.

"Oh, I think I can persuade you to part with the information." Fangs smiled. Then he pressed his lips to hers and kissed her long and hard.

115

When Milly was finally allowed up for breath, her eyes were blazing. "OK," she gasped, turning to me. "I'll tell you whatever you like. Just so long as he never does that again!"

I grinned. Sometimes my boss is the best.

Fangs cut the motorboat's engine and everything suddenly became quiet. Only the soft, rhythmic splash of water against the side of the boat broke the silence. We had arrived at a quiet bay along the coast from one of Tenerife's holiday resorts.

"This is it," I said, checking my laptop. The GPS read EL PUERTITO BAY.

"El what?" asked Fangs, peering over my shoulder.

"El Puertito," I said. "And that, over there, should be the Great Disgusto's secret hideout." I pointed to a small, seemingly deserted island in the middle distance. Milly O'Naire, who was now in jail, awaiting trial for her part in the recent robberies, had given us the precise location of Disgusto's lair in return for a single prison cell and my promise that I wouldn't let Fangs visit her.

"I wish I had my sunglasses," Fangs moaned, glancing up at the scorching sun.

When I first met my boss, I had been amazed that he could survive out in the daylight. Vampires normally shrivel up to nothing if they go out after dawn. But then I learned that Cube had invented little black pills that contained the "essence of midnight" and so long as Fangs took one every day, he was safe in the sun.

We climbed into our wetsuits – which isn't as easy as it sounds when you're covered in thick fur and have a tail. Still, it wasn't long before we each had a tank of air strapped to our back and goggles pulled down over our eyes. We sat on the side of the boat and then, on Fangs's cue, tumbled backwards into the water.

I'm always amazed at how calm and relaxed I feel when I'm scuba diving. As I swam past shoals of brightly coloured fish, I felt the tension of the last few days begin to melt away – until Fangs nudged me and pointed to a figure swimming towards us.

At first, I thought we'd found a lost wind-up bath toy. The figure's tiny legs were pumping hard, propelling it through the water like a miniature torpedo. But then I spotted the medallions hanging around its neck and realized it was Hip Hop!

With Nicolas Sizer lost in a Peruvian jungle and both Zed and Milly O'Naire behind bars, the Great Disgusto was running out of henchmen. Hip Hop may have been a small assassin, but that didn't mean getting past him would be a simple task – especially as he was holding what looked like a water pistol.

Fangs kicked his legs, aiming to get to the mini villain before he could shoot. Hip Hop's finger tightened on the trigger – but Fangs reached him just in time to pull his hand away. He twisted the gnome's wrist back, so that he couldn't shoot.

Hip Hop struggled. He thrashed from side to side, his heavy medallions churning up the water around him. Then one of Hip Hop's chains got caught in my boss's airline, wrenching it from his mouth.

Fangs spun round, desperate to locate his oxygen supply. But the only way he would be able to reach his secondary air supply was to release

Hip Hop – which would give the gnome every opportunity to aim and fire his gun.

I darted forward, pulling my mouthpiece from between my own teeth and jamming it into my boss's mouth. Fangs took a deep gulp of air and threw me a look of gratitude. At the same moment, he accidentally released his grip on Hip Hop—

Hip Hop fired his pistol.

The gun spat out an orange net with lead weights tied to each corner. As the weights spun through the water, they spread the net apart, wrapping Fangs and me in a fine mesh and dragging us down to the seabed. We both just managed to recover our mouthpieces before we crashed onto the rocks below. My foot got lodged in a wooden cage used by local fishermen to catch lobsters.

And Hip Hop wasn't finished with us yet. Taking a sharp stone from the seabed, he made a tiny cut in the tip of one of my paws. A plume of

red blood began to spiral upwards. It turned to a
crimson mist as it mixed with the water. Almost
immediately, I spotted a dark shape looming in the
distance. Then another – and another.

Sharks!

After giving us a final wicked smile, Hip Hop swam away – leaving us trapped in the net, surrounded by sharks and coated in my blood. We were an underwater packed lunch!

The sharks swam closer and closer. I pulled a knife from my utility belt and began to slice a hole in the thick netting while Fangs drank as much of the bloody water as he could.

Then one of the sharks attacked. It lunged forward, its mouth open wide and its razor-sharp teeth bared for the kill.

But it hadn't banked on meeting a vampire coming in the other direction. I cut a slit in the net for Fangs and he kicked upwards, spinning over in the water to bite the shark as hard as he could on its nose.

I'm not sure whether sharks are known for their vast array of facial expressions, but this one went from surprise, through anger, to sheer terror in a matter of seconds. It had found itself a tasty meal – but a meal with even sharper teeth than its own. Turning tail, it rocketed away through the water, closely followed by its companions.

After tearing away the rest of the net, I gave Fangs a thumbs-up. He was clamping his respirator back between his teeth. He pointed to the tiny figure swimming away from us and then drew a harpoon from the holster on his back.

For a moment I was worried that Fangs would actually shoot the gnome – he normally abhors the use of guns – but my fears were unfounded. Instead, Fangs fired the harpoon at the seabed, slicing through the rope holding a lobster net in place. The net floated upwards and caught Hip Hop as he swam. He bobbed up to the surface.

Fangs slid the harpoon back into its sheath and turned to give me a high five. We were beginning to swim in the direction of the shore when Fangs spotted one final globule of my blood. After removing his air supply again, he gulped down the red liquid, then licked the tips of his glimmering white fangs. I was suddenly very glad that we were on the same side!

We scrambled out of the water, shrugging off our scuba gear. "Do you think Hip Hop will be OK?" I asked, glancing back to where the furious gnome was shouting rhyming obscenities at us from his floating prison.

"He looks perfectly comfortable to me," said Fangs, stripping off his wetsuit. "Certainly more comfortable than whoever lives in there." He pointed further along the beach to a crudely built hut made from tree branches and dead grass.

"There's someone standing on guard outside," I hissed. "And I think he's seen us." I pulled a pair of binoculars from my utility belt and peered at the figure.

"Is it Disgusto?" asked Fangs.

I shook my head and handed the binoculars over. "I think you'd better take a look for yourself."

I climbed out of my wetsuit as Fangs was studying the figure. "What the...?" he muttered. "Come on, we need to get a better look at this."

We jogged along the beach to the hut. Its "guard" turned out to be a scarecrow dressed in a ragged pinstripe suit. Two large branches had been lashed together to form the body, and a melon, on which was drawn a scowling face with a large, handlebar moustache, was the head.

"Who's that supposed to be?" asked Fangs.

"If we weren't hundreds of miles from home, I'd say it was Sir Hugh Jands."

"The prime minister?" said Fangs. "Then who's that?" He pointed to another scarecrow.

"Could be the German chancellor," I suggested. "The seaweed looks a bit like her hairstyle."

"Well, this one just looks ridiculous!" said Fangs, striding over to a scarecrow dressed all in black. Two sharp twigs protruded from its sneering mouth and a plastic bin liner flapped from its shoulders like a cape. "I mean, who in the world looks anything like that?"

"It's you, you sabre-toothed idiot!" roared the Great Disgusto, stepping out of the ramshackle shelter.

"Rubbish!" said Fangs. "It looks nothing like me."

"Then try this..." Disgusto pulled Fangs's

sunglasses from his pocket and angrily pushed them onto the melon head.

Fangs took a step back and studied the scarecrow's new look. "OK," he admitted. "Now I can see a bit of a resemblance – but what are these things for?"

The Great Disgusto grinned wickedly. "Target practice..." He spun round, hitched up the back of his robes to reveal his golden bum and farted. A searing green flame shot out from his behind and engulfed the vampire scarecrow, melting it to a puddle of stinking goo in just a few seconds.

"As you can see," said Disgusto, dropping his robes back down, "I've made a few adjustments to my stomach agitator – with rather impressive results!"

Fangs and I stared at the hissing pool of green goo in horror. It seemed that Disgusto now had the power to destroy people with his guffs, rather than just knock them out. My boss, however, had other more pressing concerns.

"My sunglasses!" he cried, fishing in the gloop to rescue his beloved glasses, which had been reduced to nothing more than a lump of metal and glass. "You'll pay for this, Disgusto!"

"We shall see," said the Great Disgusto. "For now, though, let us relax over some light refreshments. I would ask Hip Hop to bring us some drinks, but he appears to be a little *caught* up at the moment."

I glanced at the beach hut. "That's your secret lair?"

"Hey – you wouldn't believe how much it costs to buy enough missiles to threaten the entire world," snapped Disgusto. "There wasn't much left over to build a more permanent base. Not until I organize a few more robberies, at least."

"There won't be any more robberies," said Fangs. "Or any missile attacks. It ends, here and now."

"Yes – for you!" spat the Great
Disgusto, and from his cloak he
produced two glasses of the
green stomach agitator. "Fangs
Enigma – I challenge you to a duel."

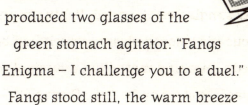

Fangs stood still, the warm breeze
ruffling his cape out behind him. "A duel?"

Disgusto nodded. "We each down a draught of
stomach agitator, then march ten paces and fart!"

Fangs's face remained blank. "You realize that
with the refinements you've made to your potion,
one of us will not survive?"

The Great Disgusto's eyes twinkled with
excitement. "That is the plan."

"Challenge accepted." Fangs took the glass and
raised the pungent drink to his lips.

I grabbed his arm. "You can't do this," I hissed.
"I don't know what the new ingredient in the
stomach agitator is yet. One mouthful of that stuff
could kill you!"

"Trust me," whispered Fangs. He waited until the Great Disgusto was looking the other way and then tipped the contents of his glass onto the ground. The liquid hissed and spat. Fangs quickly scattered sand over the puddle with his shoe to hide it.

"Well, that's something," I said with relief, "but it still doesn't mean you can match Disgusto in a bottom duel."

Fangs lifted his shirt and pulled up the waistband of his underwear. "I'm wearing these..." His boxer shorts were covered in pictures of tiny red chilli peppers.

"The chilli underpants Cube gave you!" I gasped. "Do you really think they'll give your bottom burp enough of a blast to beat Disgusto?"

"When you're ready, Agent Enigma," the Great Disgusto barked, clutching at his belly. "My agitator is beginning to churn. So if you've got the *stomach* to go through with this..."

"Bring it on, Disgusto," snarled Fangs. "You may have magic in your guts, but I've got justice in mine!"

The wizard and vampire stood back to back on the beach and then began to walk away from each other. Disgusto was counting with each step. "One ... two ... three..."

Despite the sun, I shivered. I didn't know what I would do if I lost Fangs.

"Four ... five ... six..."

Since working with Fangs at MPI, I'd been treated as an equal – not some hairy freak to be made fun of in the playground. Fangs was my best friend, and I was about to watch him die.

"Seven ... eight ... nine..."

On "nine", Fangs spun round and tossed the ball of metal and glass that had once been his favourite pair of sunglasses into the air. It glinted in the sunlight as it rose and then fell. As it came back down, Fangs kicked it as hard as he could.

"Ten!"

Twenty paces away,
the Great Disgusto pulled up his
wizard's robes, bent over and pointed his
golden bottom at my boss. He was concentrating
on guffing out the most powerful fart of his life –
when the sunglasses wedged firmly in his bum.

He turned and
his eyes flew open in
terror. The fart had
started, but now it
had nowhere to go!
Trapped inside his
body, the blast
of gas doubled
back on itself and
began to eat away
at its creator from the
inside out.

It was horrible to watch.
Disgusto flung his arms out and
screamed as his skin and flesh melted
away, leaving behind a white skeleton
wedged in the sand, the tattered remains of
the wizard's robes hanging loosely off its wasted
bones. It looked exactly like the scarecrows
Disgusto had created to stand around his hut.

His golden bottom landed in the sand with a

FLUMF!

"Now that's what I call *letting one drop*," Fangs quipped.

"That was incredible," I cried. "But you didn't use the chilli underpants?"

"You don't really think I'd trust my life to one of Cube's inventions, do you?" said Fangs with a smile.

"But how did you know the sunglasses would work?"

Fangs Enigma – the world's greatest vampire spy – arched an eyebrow. "Disgusto told us his magic was on the inside," he said. "All I had to do was keep it there!"

CASE CLOSED
SIGNED: Agent Puppy Brown

The sails of the private yacht caught the breeze and billowed out, propelling the luxury craft through the clear water. One by one, dolphins leapt from the azure surf at the head of the boat, and then dived noiselessly back beneath the surface of the water.

On the deck, a young werewolf on a sunlounger was turning a page of her book when one of her front teeth lit up blue and Fangs Enigma's voice echoed out through their private intercom.

"What do you think, Puppy?" he asked. "Didn't I tell you this would be the most relaxing way to travel home?"

Puppy Brown glanced over her shoulder to where Fangs was standing at the yacht's steering-wheel, drinking champagne with a brunette beauty in a bikini. Puppy couldn't complain about the extra company – the girl had been the sales person in Los Christianos who had taken the Great Disgusto's golden bottom in exchange for this magnificent boat. Fangs had, of course, been delighted when she had agreed to come along for the trip.

"It doesn't get better than this, boss," Puppy said, "although I could do with another orange juice." Puppy picked up a bell and rang it. A few moments later, a gnome dressed in a waiter's outfit appeared.

"Hip Hop," the werewolf said, "could I get a top up, with extra ice this time?"

The gnome swore beneath his breath. *"Yo, yo,"* he rapped. *"You can't order me around. Can't tell me what to do. Can't make me serve you. And the vampire too!"*

Puppy smiled sweetly. "Actually, we can. We offered you a deal, remember? Work your passage back to the UK and go free, or don't and we'll stick you in a cell at MP1 Headquarters with Zed."

Hip Hop swallowed his anger and picked up Puppy's empty glass.

The werewolf had just settled back into her book when her tooth lit up blue again.

"Agent Brown," gurgled the voice of Phlem. "Where are you? I was expecting you back at HQ this morning."

Puppy glanced up at Fangs and his new friend and smiled. "Agent Engima needs time to question a new witness, so we're taking the long way home."

"Very well," grumbled the slime beast. "I just wanted to make sure that you and Fangs had wrapped up the case with the Great Disgusto."

"We got to the *bottom* of it, sir," said Puppy. "And it was a *stinker*!"

TEST YOUR SECRET-AGENT

Spot the Difference (There are eight to spot.)

SKILLS WITH THESE PUZZLES!

Fart Facts

Do you know these guff-tastic fart facts?

Which animals are the fartiest on the planet?

A) Cows

B) Termites

C) Flamingos

Can you name a couple of animals that don't fart at all?

Fart Facts

Many people believe that cows fart the most, but in fact termites pass more gas. (We don't know how much flamingos fart – perhaps you can do some research and find out!) Camels, zebras and sheep are also parp-tastic.

Creatures that don't parp include sponges, jellyfish and some types of worm.

Answers

UNLOCK SECRET MISSION FILES!

Want to gain access to highly classified MP1 files? Complete the crossword below, and then enter the password (the letters in the grey boxes) at

WWW.FANGSVAMPIRESPY.CO.UK/MISSION1

Across

2. What type of food appears on Cube's gadget underpants? (6)
4. Who is the head of MP1? (5)
6. What does Puppy find on Hip Hop's cap? (3)
8. Name a type of mushroom. Hint: it's mentioned in this book. (8)
10. What is Puppy's favourite drink? (6, 5)

Down

1. What is the Great Disgusto's dentist called? (7, 5)
3. Name Disgusto's mini henchman. (3, 3)
5. What fish are in Disgusto's pool? (7)
7. Where is the casino? (5, 5)
9. What does Fangs use to defeat Disgusto? (10)
11. What colour is Zed's boat? (5)
12. Who is the British prime minister in the Fangs books? (4, 5)